STALKED BY THE LAWYER

EMMA BRAY

Logan

MY FOOTSTEPS RESONATE against the stone as I approah one of my wealthiest client's door.

The mansion looms before me, its presence imposing under the cloak of twilight. It's an architectural master-piece, with soaring columns that stand like sentinels guarding the secrets within. This house, with its manicured gardens and a facade kissed by moon-light, whispers of old money and quiet power.

I pause at the double oak doors, their intricate carvings a testament to the grandeur beyond. My fingers graze over the brass knocker, feeling the cool metal against my skin. With a practiced motion, I announce my arrival, the sound sharp in the crisp evening air.

The door swings open, and I step over the threshold into this world of elegance. Shadows dance across marble floors, and chandeliers glitter from above, casting prisms of light that flicker like stars fallen from the heavens.

The door's echo fades as my gaze lifts to meet my client. He stands before me, a figure carved from the same stern granite as his home. His handshake is an iron clamp, unyielding and cold—a silent assertion of dominance.

"Logan," he says, voice deep like the rumble of distant thunder. "Come in."

I step forward, the air shifting around me as I cross into his domain. No corner of this grand foyer escapes the meticulous touch of affluence. It's a vault of treasures where even the silence seems expensive.

Well, my clients *are* rich, and that's what makes me my money.

To my right, a grand staircase sweeps upward, its banister gleaming with the polish of careful hands. Above, a crystal chandelier presides like a crown jewel, each facet meticulously placed to scatter light across the expanse of marble below.

"Beautiful, isn't it?" Mr. Brimming's voice cuts through my reverie, a note of pride threading the otherwise stoic delivery.

"Indeed," I reply, my words measured, careful not to betray too much admiration. This chessboard of luxury is impressive, but I never let my clients know my real feelings—on anything.

In the spaces between shadows and light, ornate paintings watch over us, their subjects dressed in layers of historical finery. They whisper stories of legacy and time, of wealth passed down through generations. The furniture echoes this narrative. Each piece is a masterwork, from the plush velvet settees to the dark mahogany tables, all poised with aristocratic grace.

"Your collection is remarkable," I comment, knowing full well each item has been chosen to impress, to intimidate.

"Collected over many years," he replies, his tone dismissive, as if the effort to amass such splendor was nothing more than a trivial pastime.

I nod, allowing a brief smile to show my respect for the game he plays. Power resides here, not just in the tangible opulence, but in the unseen currents that run beneath the surface,

"Shall we begin?" I suggest.

"Of course." He turns, leading the way, and I follow, my senses sharpened. Clients don't hire me for no reason. He's hiding something, but he'll pay me to clean up his mess.

We pore over his documents for at least an air before the air shifts. I look up and my gaze locks onto...my god, she's the most beautiful creature I've ever seen. Long red hair that waves down her back. Big green eyes framed by thick, dark lashes. And holy fuck. Puffy pink lips that would make a sex doll envious.

I feel myself harden in my pants and shift to hide my growing erection. What the fuck? How can one look at this girl have me harder than I've been in years?

This flame-haired enigma holds more sway over me than she can possibly fathom.

"Ah, Logan, I'd like you to meet Jill, my daughter. Jill, come here for a minute."

She steps into the light, an ethereal vision against the backdrop of her father's fortress. Her fiery red hair is an untamed cascade, a vibrant contrast to the muted opulence around us. It frames her face, a masterpiece painted with the softest brushstrokes of beauty—a beauty that doesn't beg but commands attention.

In that instant, as our eyes lock, it's as if the very pulse of the room synchronizes with mine. *Electrified.* A magnetic storm swirls between us, silent and unseen but potent enough to send shockwaves through the soles of my shoes. There's a gravity to her presence, pulling me into an orbit I have no desire to break free from.

Her curious gaze sweeps to me as he father introduces me.

"Hello, Logan," she breathes out my name, and it's not just a greeting but an incantation, imbuing the syllables with a power that resonates deep within my chest.

"Jill." The word is a caress, spoken with a reverence reserved for sacred things, for desires whispered in the dark.

We stand there, the space between us charged with the unsaid—the unyielding tension of want colliding with the impossibility of the situation. She's the flame, and I'm too enthralled to consider the searing consequence of getting too close. But oh, how I yearn to be burnt by that fire.

The world resumes its spin, the murmur of Brimming's voice filters back, but it's just a shadow at the edge of my consciousness. My focus remains laser-sharp on the woman before me, the one who has become the fulcrum of my every waking thought.

"Stunning" would be too tame a word to capture the essence of Jill as she stands there, a testament to living art. There's an allure that goes beyond the visual, something elemental that speaks to the core of who I am.

I finally clear my throat and speak to her again. "Your father mentioned your interest in corporate law," I begin, threading common ground into the fabric of our interaction. "It's a ruthless arena."

"Ruthless, but intellectually stimulating," she counters, her lips curving into a smile that promises intrigue. "Don't you think?"

"Absolutely," I concede, the words smooth as silk across my tongue. "A chess game where the stakes are real. And every move is critical."

"Then you appreciate strategy," Jill muses, tilting her head slightly, her red hair catching the light like flames licking at the edges of my restraint.

"Strategy, and the occasional surprise maneuver." I let my gaze drop momentarily to her lips, then back up to meet her eyes, a silent acknowledgment of the game we're now playing.

"Surprises can be... exhilarating," she whispers, leaning in just enough for me to catch the hint of her perfume, a scent that beckons me closer to danger's edge.

"Like finding an unexpected ally in a battlefield," I say, mirroring her lean, closing the space between us. Our conversation feels like a dance, one where every step is measured, every turn anticipated yet thrilling.

"Or an adversary worthy of one's respect," she adds, those emerald eyes sparkling with the challenge she presents.

"Respect," I echo, feeling the weight of the word, knowing it carries far more than its surface meaning between us.

"Perhaps even... admiration?" Her eyebrow arches, a silent dare woven into her casual inquiry.

"Admiration," I acknowledge, "and fascination. It's a potent combination."

"Potent enough to be dangerous," she says softly, a truth wrapped in velvet.

"Only if one isn't prepared to handle it." I reach out, my fingers brushing against hers in a fleeting caress masquerading as an accidental touch.

"Are you?" The question hangs in the air, laced with the promise of secrets yet to be shared.

"Am I ever," I reply, the corner of my mouth lifting in a half-smile that speaks volumes.

Our connection simmers, a fusion of intellect and raw desire, each word exchanged another layer peeled back in the intricate dance of discovery. With every glance, every subtle gesture, the draw between us pulls tighter, a magnetic force neither willing nor able to resist.

Brimming beams at us. "Jill's only nineteen," he informs me, "but she's already well on her way to being accepted to the most prestigious law school in the nation. Isn't that right, honey?"

She smiles graciously and shrugs.

The clock chimes, a somber reminder that it's high time I get out of her. However, as I stand to take my leave, every fiber of my being resists the motion. "I should get going," I say, voice low, each syllable laced with reluctance.

"Of course," Brimming replies, but I don't even spare him another glance. I'm too busy watching his daughter as she rises gracefully from her seat, the light casting shadows across her features that only enhance her allure.

I turn toward the door, but not before my gaze lingers on her one last time. The way she stands there, amid the opulence of her surroundings, yet outshining it all with the sheer force of her presence—it sears itself into my memory. Her fiery hair frames her face, a wild and untamed halo, and her eyes, luminous and penetrating, hold me captive without even trying.

"Logan," she breathes out, and I swear a drop of precum shoots out of my tip and stains the insides of my trousers.

"Jill." Her name is a caress on my lips, a whisper of longing. For a moment, we stand locked in a silent exchange, words unnecessary when our eyes are speaking volumes.

"Mr. Brimming," I nod to her father sharply before I pivot on my heel. With each step away from her, an inferno of desire rages within me, threatening to consume any semblance of restraint I have left.

Outside, the night air bites at my skin, a stark contrast to the warmth I'm leaving behind. I descend the steps of her father's mansion, each footfall heavy with the weight of unspoken promises and smoldering intent.

As I slip into the driver's seat of my car, I can't shake the image of Jill from my mind's eye. In the rearview mirror, I catch the reflection of her house, lights ablaze, a beacon in the darkness, much like she is in my world—dazzling and dangerous.

The engine roars to life, a growl that mirrors the storm brewing inside me. My hands grip the steering wheel, knuckles turning white, as I fight the urge to rush back inside, consequences be damned.

The road blurs, a streak of inky black beneath the glow of a crescent moon. Each mile I put between myself and Jill's father's house tightens the knot of desire coiled in my gut. My hands grip the steering wheel, knuckles white, as if holding on to the last vestiges of self-control.

I can't shake her image—the way her hair shimmered like a halo of flames, the laughter that seemed to dance in her eyes just for me. It clings to the edge of my mind, a ghostly presence that refuses to fade into the night.

"Focus," I chastise myself, forcing my thoughts away from the dangerous curve of her lips. But even as I do, there's an undercurrent of exhilaration that pulses through me.

She's only nineteen, for fuck's sake, and I'm thirty. She's way too young for me. What's more is she's the daughter of my most influential—and dangerous—

client. I'd be a fool to get involved with her.

At a red light, I pause, and the world seems to hold its breath with me. The digital glow of the dashboard clock marks the passing seconds.

"Logan," I remember the ways she whispered my name like a prayer. It's etched into my brain, a brand upon my consciousness.

The light shifts to green, propelling me forward. I navigate the sleeping city, a concrete jungle with its own set of laws—laws that I'm adept at bending to my will. Yet, as I approach my apartment, the sanctuary where I usually find solace in solitude, there's a restlessness that claws at me.

As I turn the key in my lock, the familiar click feels like the closing of a cell door. The space greets me with shadow and silence, but I can almost sense her here, a phantom woven from my own longing.

I pour a drink, the liquid amber catching the scant light, and take a slow sip. The burn down my throat does little to temper the heat that Jill ignited in me. I move to the window, peering out over the cityscape, a kingdom of glass and steel.

"Jill," I say her name aloud this time, testing the power it holds, rolling it around in my mouth like a forbidden fruit. It tastes of danger and seduction—a potent combination.

I set the glass down, the clink of it against the countertop sharp in the quiet. I should be strategizing, plotting my next move in the high-stakes case that brought us together. Instead, I find my fingers tracing patterns on the cool surface, doodling destinies that can never be.

"Control," I remind myself once more. But it's a feeble attempt at reclaiming the ground that's slipping beneath me. The pull toward her is gravitational, and fighting it requires an effort that borders on the impossible.

My cock is still aching, and I finally stop fighting it.

I drop my pants and grasp my hard length, my hand flying up and down it, my eyes shut tight as I imagine Jill's puffy pink lips wrapped around me.

I think of her red hair, her eyes, the way she moves. I imagine that way she would suck on the tip tentatively, her eyes looking up into mine. Would her pussy get wet?

The thought of her sweet pussy, wet and glistening is what finally does it. I come with a harsh grunt and then collapse onto my bed, panting for breath as if I've just run a marathon.

Fuuuck.

CHAPTER
TWO

Logan

I'M in the back row again, eyes fixed on her red hair catching the afternoon sun through the windows. Jill's head is tilted down, pen scribbling notes, and I imagine she's writing a secret message to me. My fingers twitch with the urge to run through those strands, to feel their silk against my skin.

I swallow hard, tension coiling inside me. It's been days since I last touched myself, thinking of her, her name a whispered prayer on my lips as I come undone. I cling to these moments like a lifeline, the hunger for her gnawing at my insides until it's all-consuming.

After class, I follow at a distance, my gaze locked on the sway of her hips. It's pathetic, I know. I thirty-year-old successful lawyer sitting in on college classes for the chance at a mere glimpse of a college student, but god help me, I can't help myself.

She laughs with friends, her voice a melody that I chase like a drug. They're headed to some café, and I slip into the crowd behind them, shadowing her every step. She's oblivious to my presence, to the heat of my stare burning into her back.

I check her social media feed again, thumb flicking over the screen. There she is, smiling out from a dozen photos, each one a shard of ice piercing deeper into my chest. Her digital footprint is a map, and I'm the silent stalker charting every course, every like, every comment she makes.

My phone buzzes with her latest

update—a picture, her face glowing with laughter—and my response is visceral, immediate. In the privacy of my home, I give in to the fantasies that plague me, my hand a poor substitute for the warmth of her flesh.

"Fuck," I curse under my breath, the afterglow tinged with a bitter longing. It's not enough. It will never be enough until she's mine.

***

My pulse hammers as I watch Jill slip into the lecture hall, her laughter a silken thread winding around my gut, pulling tight. I'm perched on the third floor balcony of the neighboring building, eyes trained on the doorway she just vanished through. She's unaware of me, but I'm so attuned to her that I can almost feel the brush of her body heat against my skin from here.

Every glance, every smile she shares with those around her—it's like a knife twisting in my chest. They don't know her—not like I do. Not like I need to. My desire for her is a living thing, coiled inside me, growing bigger and hungrier with each passing day.

I should be preparing for my next case, but instead, I'm here at this fucking college campus I have no business being at, consumed by thoughts of her. It's reckless, this game of proximity I play, edging closer to the fire when I know it'll burn. But God, I crave the heat, the danger. It makes me feel alive in ways nothing else has.

"Control yourself," I mutter under my breath, a mantra that's lost its meaning. I've repeated it so many times it's become nothing more than background noise. Yet, the idea of touching her, of claiming her as mine—it's a compulsion that overrides logic, reason, even self-preservation.

I force myself to leave before the class ends, to maintain the facade of a man who has his shit together. But it's a lie—a thin veneer over the chaos she stirs within me. I'm a lawyer, for fuck's sake. I have a reputation, a career that could crumble if I cross that line. And yet, the risk adds a sick thrill to the fantasy.

"Fuck," I say again, the word slipping out like a prayer or a curse—I can't tell which anymore. The thought of her soft curves beneath my hands, her gasp of surprise turning into moans of pleasure...it's maddening. She's poison and antidote all rolled into one, and I'm addicted to the taste I've never had.

I'm back in my office now, door locked, blinds drawn. The image of her today—how her skirt clung to her thighs, how her hair fell over her shoulder—plays on a loop in my mind. I lean back in my chair, hand slipping beneath the waistband of my slacks. I close my eyes, and it's her hand, not mine, that I imagine. Her touch, her breath against my neck.

"Jill," I breathe out her name like it's a sacred incantation, as my body tenses, reaching for a release that's as much pain as it is pleasure. There's no stopping this, no going back. I'm falling, spiraling, losing myself to this obsession.

And deep down, I know I'm past the point of no return.

***

The phone buzzes in my pocket, a vibration that ripples through me like an electric shock. It's him, Jill's father—her patriarchal gatekeeper holding the keys to my damnation.

"Logan," he says, his voice like gravel on the line, "I've got a favor to ask you."

My heart thumps—a feral drumbeat in my chest as I wait for it, the request I didn't know I was praying for until this moment.

"Jill's struggling a bit with her college courses," he continues. "Could use a tutor. I immediately thought of you. You're sharp, Logan, and hell, she's going into the same field as you. Thought you could help her out."

Every word pulses through me, ignites something dark and hungry. Tutoring Jill. Alone time with her. The idea is a spark thrown into the dry tinder of my obsession.

"Sure," I say, voice steady despite the

tempest inside me. "I'd be happy to help." Happy is a euphemism for ecstatic, for desperate, for fucking starving.

"Great. I'll let her know you'll reach out to set up a time."

"Of course," I reply, before ending the call, my breaths coming out short, ragged. This is what I want, isn't it? The chance to be near her, to bask in the glow of her presence without the pretense of accidental encounters.

But there's a coil of anxiety in the pit of my stomach, tight and cold. How am I supposed to keep my hands to myself, my thoughts pure when every second with her will be a test of restraint?

My reflection in the phone screen sneers back at me. I'm playing with fire, walking a razor's edge between professionalism and the raw, primal urge to claim her.

I picture those tutoring sessions, just the two of us, cloistered in some quiet corner of the library or at her room, delving into textbooks and notes. Her brow furrowed in concentration, biting her lip in frustration, looking up at me with those wide, innocent eyes for help. And God, how I'll want to help—want to teach her more than just the curriculum, want to educate her in the language of sighs and moans, in the give and take of flesh on flesh.

It's dangerous, this game I'm about to play. But the thrill of it courses through my veins like a drug I'm too far gone to quit. I can already feel the heat of her skin beneath my fingertips, the sweet torture of maintaining control when every fiber of my being screams to take her, make her *mine*.

Tonight, I'll lay awake, wrestling with the dual forces of anticipation and dread churning inside me. Tomorrow, I'll face her with a smile plastered on my face and a monster caged behind my ribs.

***

The clock ticks—a metronome to my skyrocketing pulse as I wait for her at the library's private study room. The door creaks open, and there she is.

Jill, with her cascade of auburn hair and that oblivious smile that could damn or save me at any given moment.

"Hey, Logan," she greets, and the sound of my name on her lips feels like a caress I don't deserve.

"Hey." My voice is a strangled sort of gruffness, betraying none of the chaos she ignites within me.

We sit across from each other at the small table, textbooks and notes forming a paper barricade between us. But it's futile. The air is thick with unspoken words and unacted deeds, a tension that weaves around us like a tangible web.

"Let's start with the corporate law," I suggest, trying to steer my mind towards academic banality. "Jump right into it, wouldn't you say?"

"Absolutely," she nods, flipping open her textbook with slender fingers that I envision tracing patterns not on parchment but on skin—my skin.

We dive into the material, but the undercurrent of our exchanges isn't lost on me. Every brush of her hand against mine while passing a pen, every shared glance when we decipher a particularly tricky passage—it's foreplay masked as tutoring, and I'm drowning in the subtext.

"Your father tells me you paint," I comment during a lull, watching her eyes light up.

"Yeah, I do. It's like... letting out a breath I didn't know I was holding." Her words float between us, laden with vulnerability.

"I know the feeling," I confess, and it's true. The darkness inside me recognizes the need to create, to channel what simmers beneath the surface into something tangible.

"Logan?" Her gaze holds mine, earnest and piercing. "What do you do to let go?"

"Exercise," I lie smoothly, a half-truth. Because the full truth involves images of her, spun in the privacy of my mind, unraveling me until I am raw and exposed.

"Good for you," she smiles, unaware that she's the core of my nightly exertions, the unwitting muse of my self-inflicted torment.

"Thank you for doing this, Logan," Jill says as we wrap up, oblivious to the storm she stirs within me. "I feel like I understand this stuff so much better now."

"Anytime," I manage to say, even as I stand on the precipice of control, peering into the abyss that yawns wide at the thought of being her anytime, all the time.

"See you Thursday?" she asks, packing up her bag.

"Thursday," I confirm, the word a tether I cling to as she leaves, taking the warmth of her presence with her.

Alone, the silence of the room echoes the roar in my veins. I close my eyes, replaying every moment, every innocent touch and shared confession, sealing them away like contraband treasures.

And I pull my aching cock out and jack off furiously. It's the only thing that keeps me sane.

Logan

ON AND ONE WE GO, week after week, and it gets harder and harder to tutor her without touching her. She scoots her chair closer to mine, looks up at me with those big, innocent eyes, worries that puffy pink lip between her teeth.

"Logan?" she calls me back to the present. She's asking me another quesiton, but I didn't hear a word of it, so lost in my fantasties of her. My cock is rock hard and leaking a constant stream of precum. I don't know how much longer I can go on like this.

"What was the question?" I ask her as I take in her angelic face. God, she's beautiful.

And then before I realize what I'm doing, I lean in, my lips a breath away from hers. The air crackles with the electricity of forbidden desires, and I'm a man parched, standing before an oasis that promises both life and death. Her eyes are wide, dark pools of innocence that beckon me to drown in their depths.

"Logan..." she whispers, a tentative hand reaching up to brush against my cheek. It's the spark that ignites the wildfire within me.

I crash into her, my hands threading through her hair as I claim her mouth with mine. She gasps, a small sound swallowed by the urgency of our kiss. This is it—the moment of surrender. I can't hold back any longer. I'm consumed by the ravenous beast of my own longing.

Her back presses against the wall of

my place, the plaster cold and unyield-ing, a stark contrast to the heat of our bodies intertwined. I think I knew this was going to happen—at least I secretly wanted it to. That's why I started inviting her here to my place for our tutoring sessions. I wanted to be able to smell her long after she left, see her everywhere I looked.

Her fingers dig into my shoulders, pulling me closer, and I lose myself in the sensation of her soft curves yielding to my hardened edges.

"Jill," I groan against her neck, my voice hoarse with want. My hands explore, memorizing every inch of her, claiming territory in a land I have no right to conquer. The taste of her skin is intoxicating, a heady mix of sweat and sweetness that drives me wild.

"Fuck, baby. Do you know how long I've wanted this?" The confession tumbles from me unbidden as I run my fingers along her hard nipples.

"Me too," she pants, her voice a wanton invitation that spurs me on.

We're a tangle of limbs and

discarded clothes, our lesson in corporate law long forgotten as we delve into the murky waters of lust and desire. I break away, teasingly tracing a line down her abdomen with my tongue.

"Logan," she moans, and the sound of her pleasure is both agony and ecstasy. I can't get enough of her—her taste, her scent, the way she trembles under my touch.

My hand finds her heat, slick and ready for me. "God, you're so wet for me, Jill." I can't help but praise her as I tease her clit with my fingertips.

"Yes," she moans as she gasps.

"Tell me, has a man ever touched you like this before?" I ask her.

Her cheeks turn pink as she shakes her head. "No."

That confession makes precum froth from my tip. "Fuck," I groan as every cell in my body demands I claim her and make her mine. Only *mine*.

My mouth falls between her legs as I taste her sweetness for the first time. She jumps, her fingers tangling in my hair as she pushes her pussy deeper into my face.

Holy fuck.

"More," she breathes out, a plea that shatters the last of my restraint. I rip our clothing from us and position myself at her core.

"Look at me demand. I need to see those pretty eyes when I make you mine."

She bites her lip, her green eyes locked onto mine.

"That's a good girl," I praise her as I slip inside her hot heat for the first time. She's so tight and wet that it's all I can do to not instantly nut inside her.

"Damn, baby. Gripping me so tight with that little virgin cunt. You have no idea how good you feel to me right now."

She whimpers and raises her hips, trying to readjust on me, but she only makes me slide deeper.

I groan as she cries out, and then I lose control. I start to fuck into her hard and fast and furious.

I worship her body with mine, each thrust a promise.

"God, Jill, you feel so good," I grunt out between thrusts.

Her nails dig into my back as she comes undone beneath me, screaming my name like a prayer.

My eyes roll back in my head as I finally fall over the edge. I spray my cum inside her, the thought of filling her up with my seed only making me come that much harder.

Our shuddering climax leaves us clinging to each other.

I'm never letting her go.

EPILOGUE

Ten Years Later

Jill

THE DOOR CLICKS SHUT behind us. My heart pounds as Logan turns the lock, sealing us in our new office. His gaze meets mine, smoldering intensity burning in his eyes.

Fuck, I love these games we play. I graduated from law school, and we started our our practice. We're our own bosses, so we can fuck—and suck—as much as we want.

He stalks towards me, hunger etched into every line of his body. I back up until I hit the edge of the desk, hands gripping the wood behind me.

"Jill." My name is a rough groan on his lips. He closes the distance between us, pulling me into his arms. His mouth crashes onto mine, hot and demanding, devouring me whole.

I moan into the kiss, arching against him. His hands are everywhere at once, clutching my ass, tangling in my hair, sliding under my shirt to caress my skin.

We stumble backwards and papers scatter, pens rolling across the floor. Logan lifts me onto the desk, shoving my skirt up around my waist. I wrap my legs around him, dragging him closer.

He tears his mouth from mine, lips and teeth tracing a burning path down my neck. "So perfect" His voice is a dark rumble against my skin. "You keep my cock hard, baby."

Heat pools low in my belly at his words.

A growl rumbles in his chest. He

captures my mouth again in a bruising kiss as his hands slide between us, unbuckling his belt.

I'm trembling with need, aching for him, but I want to please him first, so I slide to my knees, peeking up at him as I do so.

He hisses in a sharp breath as he realizes my intention. "Fuck yes," he breathes.

He groans as I take him into my mouth, hands clutching the edge of the desk. I swirl my tongue around the head of his cock, tasting the saltiness of his arousal, before sinking down and taking him deep.

He curses under his breath, hips thrusting forward. I place my hands on his thighs to hold him still, setting a slow, torturous pace. I want to draw this out, to give him as much pleasure as possible. To prove how much I want this, want him.

I glance up through my lashes and see him watching me, eyes dark with lust, chest heaving. "Fuck, Jill." His voice is strained. "Your mouth..."

I hum in satisfaction, the vibrations eliciting another groan from him. His fingers tangle in my hair, gripping tight, trying to urge me on, faster and deeper, but I resist. I'm in control here. I'm going to take my time.

Logan is usually so dominant, always in control, but not now. Not with me. I have him at my mercy, coming undone under my touch. The knowledge thrills me, spurs me on. I slide one hand between his legs to cup his balls, squeezing gently, as I take him all the way into my throat.

"Jesus!" His hips jerk forward and he throws his head back, fingers tightening in my hair. I can tell he's close, can feel his body tensing, hear his breath coming in ragged gasps.

I'm going to make him come undone, just for me.

But then, he suddenly pulls me up from the floor, hands roaming over my body as if he can't get enough of me. Our kiss is hungry, desperate, all teeth and tongue. I moan into his mouth, arching against him, needing to feel his skin on mine.

He breaks away suddenly and spins me around, bending me over the desk. My heart races in anticipation. Knowing what he's about to do to me makes me so wet I can feel it dripping down my thighs.

Logan kneels behind me, trailing kisses up the back of my legs. When he reaches my core, he groans. "So fucking wet for me." His tongue circles my clit and I cry out, gripping the edge of the desk to stay upright. The sensation is almost too much to bear, spiraling pleasure and pain.

He slides one finger inside me, then two, stretching and stroking as he continues to lavish attention on my clit. I'm panting, shaking, hovering on the edge of release. "Please," I gasp.

Logan chuckles softly, the vibrations shooting through me. "Not yet, baby." He quickens the pace of his fingers, curling them to hit just the right spot. "Come for me, Jill. I want to feel you come all over my fingers."

His words push me over and I shatter, crying out his name as waves of pleasure crash over me. Logan works me through my orgasm, prolonging the ecstasy, before finally withdrawing his fingers and standing.

I'm still trembling, heart pounding, when I feel the head of his cock at my entrance. "Ready for more?" he murmurs, gripping my hips.

I look over my shoulder at him, eyes heavy-lidded. "God yes."

Logan slides into me with agonizing slowness, stretching me inch by inch. We moan in unison, savoring the feeling of becoming one. When he's fully seated inside me, he pauses, leaning over to kiss the back of my neck.

"You feel so fucking good," he whispers against my skin. He begins to move, slow thrusts that make my toes curl. The desk creaks beneath us, papers and pens scattering to the floor, but I don't care. All that matters is Logan and the exquisite pleasure he's giving me.

He straightens, quickening his pace, and grips my hips to pull me back onto his cock. I cry out at the new angle, even deeper than before. Logan grunts with each thrust, the sound primal and intoxicating.

The pressure begins to build again, simmering heat in my core. I rock back to meet his thrusts, our bodies moving as one. Logan reaches around to rub my clit in tight circles and I shatter again, vision going white.

Logan's thrusts pound into me, intense and unrelenting.

"Jill," Logan groans. "Come with me."

His words push me over and I shatter around him, crying out his name.

He fucks me through my orgasm, chasing his own release. His thrusts become erratic, grip on my hips bruising, as he finds his climax. He stills, burying himself to the hilt, and groans my name. I feel the pulses of his cock inside me, claiming me as his.

We collapse onto the desk, a tangle of sweaty limbs and harsh breaths. Logan kisses my shoulder, nuzzling against my neck. "I love you," he murmurs.

I smile, basking in the afterglow and his words. "I love you too."

Want a free book from Emma Bray? Go to www.authoremmabray.com.

Keep reading for an excerpt from Secrets:

Chapter 1

Zane

My name is Zane Culvert, and I have a secret. Well, two secrets, actually.

My first secret?

I know all of Anne Johnson's secrets.

I know that her mother sent her to kindergarten a year early just to get her out of her hair while she fucked the johns that paid her rent.

I know that because of that, Anne was always the youngest and smallest one in her class and that she always felt left behind and mostly stuck to herself throughout grade school.

I know that she threw herself into her studies, graduated early, and started attending college at seventeen instead of eighteen, hence why she's the youngest fully licensed elementary school teacher in the city.

I know that she's really the face behind Charlotte Locke, the famed naughty romance novelist.

I know that despite her erotic writings, Anne is really a virgin.

Thank God for that. Really, it saves me a lot of time and aggravation. I don't have a list of men to kill now. She really did the world a service by retaining her innocence.

I know that she still feels guilty about her mother's death. It wasn't her fault at all, but she feels like she should have done more, sat with her more in the hospital as the cancer at away at her body.

That's natural guilt, I suppose. When someone you love dies, you'll always feel like you didn't do enough, like there was more you could have done—no matter how much you did.

That's what I've heard anyway. I don't know from firsthand experience seeing as how I've never cared for anyone enough to care when they died.

One of my many character flaws, I suppose. A lack of empathy, the psychologists had called it.

Makes me perfect for working the unsavory jobs I do on the streets, dealing with the dregs of society.

But the nature of my work isn't my second secret.

No, my second secret?

My second secret is this: Anne Johnson is my obsession. I watch her every second of the motherfucking day.

I've been watching her for two years now. I suppose "stalking" is the technical term for what I'm doing, but I don't like to call it that.

Stalking sounds so…devious, calculated.

And while I am those things—and frequently—that's not the case when I watch Anne.

When I watch Anne, I *feel*.

I feel so many things. Despair, desire, lust, pain, anxiety, fear. I feel more than I've ever felt in my pitiful excuse for an existence.

She gives me a reason to exist. Watching her, protecting her, guarding her from afar. She is my purpose in this life.

Anne Johnson is my everything.

And she doesn't even know it.

I've thought of approaching her many times. God knows how much I long to take her in my arms, hold her against me, run my fingers through her auburn hair and along her milky white skin just to see if she's as soft as she looks.

I want to cherish her, see her smile, be the cause of her smile, feel her light shining down on me. Have her blue eyes peering up at me behind those tortoiseshell cat-eye glasses she wears.

I would die of happiness at just one look from her.

This feeling that grips my chest and tightens it every time I think of her—much less look at her…

I don't know what to call it. I've determined that it must be "love." Something I never thought myself capable of feeling. I'm still not entirely sure I'm capable of it.

And there are so many definitions of it, depending upon who you ask. All I know is that I feel like I'll die if I don't see her every day, that I'd give my life to protect her.

I'm perfectly content to sit and watch her sleeping for hours.

I've got cameras rigged up all throughout her apartment. I have a tracking device on her phone. I frequently sneak into her apartment and read her diary, catching up on all the thoughts in my beautiful little Annie's head.

That's what I call her secretly.

My little Annie.

There's nothing I'd rather read than her innermost thoughts. Some might call me breaking into her apartment, reading her diary, and keeping tabs on her everywhere she goes an invasion of privacy, but I can't help it. Everything about her fascinates me.

I feel closer to her than anyone else on this entire planet.

And she doesn't even know I exist.

I stroke my finger over her face on my phone screen where I have my live camera feed of her pulled up.

She's curled up on her side, her hands in little balls under her chin as she slumbers peacefully.

Like a pretty little kitten.

When did I "meet" her?

It was monumental and yet it wasn't. Nothing super big happened and yet it did. What I mean is there weren't any extraordinary circumstances that led to our encounter.

I was just jogging through the park one day, doing my regular routine.

It was starting to rain. People were

hauling ass to get back to their apartments, but I was enjoying my run.

A little rain never hurt me. In fact, I like it when it rains because then the park clears completely out. I get a sick sense of satisfaction at watching all the park-goers scurry away like mice seeking shelter.

I rounded the bend in the track, and there she was.

She was several feet up ahead just sitting on a park bench serenely.

Completely unbothered by the fact that she was getting drenched.

Her eyes were closed, her face slightly tilted up as if she welcomed the droplets on her face, the wet waves of hair plastered against her cheeks, neck, shoulders, and arms. The little gold dress she had on was plastered against her skin, wet against her creamy thighs that were glistening with water.

She looked peaceful and yet sad all at the same time. Something about the vision she presented wrapped its fingers around my neck, cutting off all my air. I couldn't breathe there for a moment.

And for the first time in my life, I couldn't move.

I stopped dead in my tracks and just stared at her.

I'd never seen anything more beautiful. And I'm not just talking about her physical beauty.

No, it was more than that.

It was her soul, her aura, her essence, whatever the fuck you want to call it.

It was breathtakingly, heart-stoppingly beautiful.

I don't know how long she just sat there in her own little world, her eyes closed. I don't know how long I stood there staring at her, but I eventually got my wits about me enough to move off to a line of trees where I could continue to watch her undetected.

From that moment on, I followed her. I found out everything I could about her. I've shamelessly manipulated circumstances so that I can keep an eye on her at all times.

And the more I found out about her, the tighter my chest got, the deeper my obsession grew, until I'm drowning it.

But I don't want to be saved. I want to drown in her.

I keep telling myself that this is enough. Watching her is enough.

I know I could easily slip into her apartment while she's there, satiate my longing to feel her skin and run a hand along her hair and cheek while she sleeps.

But I don't. I know that one taste of her will undo me.

If I touch her one time, I don't think I'll ever be able to let her go.

And I'm not worthy of her. I'm darkness, and she's the purest light. My hands are dirty, and I don't want to taint her with all that I am.

But, fuck, how I long for her.

I pull my dick out of my joggers and begin stroking it quickly while I stare down at the screen. I hold the hair scrunch I grabbed from her apartment up to my nose and inhale deeply.

Oh fuck.

Her sweet raspberry scent fills my nostrils just as I come, shooting sticky ropes up onto my stomach with a grunt.

All it takes is her scent to send me over the edge. If I ever had my cock actually inside her, I'd probably die.

Or at the very least embarrass myself by ejaculating immediately like an overeager teenage boy.

My phone buzzes, and I regretfully close out of the camera feed of my little Annie to check the incoming text.

Unsurprisingly, it's a client wanting another "favor."

I pocket my phone as I rise and get ready to go to work. Even though I know she'll be sleeping, I can't go more than a few hours without having to check the feed to check on her.

Until tomorrow, my sweet little Annie.

Chapter 2

Anne

My name is Anne Johnson, and I have a secret. Actually, I have a lot of secrets, the biggest being that I write dirty romance novels in my free time.

I write under a pen name, of course. We can't have the city finding out the person behind the steamy Charlotte Locke novels is actually an elementary school teacher.

That probably wouldn't go over well with the parents or the board.

Especially since my heroines are usually always virgins, and my heroes are alpha males who take what they want. *The Romance Digest* has rated my book's sex scenes with five peppers, the spiciest sizzle rating you can get.

Want to know what's ironic about that?

I've never had sex.

I'm still a virgin.

Yep. A twenty-two-year-old virgin.

I don't really have a clue what I'm talking about. Yes, I understand the mechanics of sex, and a well-described sex scene can get my panties wet and my pulse racing.

But I've never had an orgasm.

I don't truly know what I'm writing

about when I write about that white-hot release. I'm only saying what the characters tell me to say.

Imagine the world's shock if everyone found out that I, a virgin who has no first-hand experience with sex whatsoever, is the one churning out such realistic sex scenes.

Imagine what the parents and board members would say if they knew that I'm the one writing what they would no doubt deem as filth.

But here's the thing. They're all hypocrites because according to the astronomical sums I get from my royalties, someone is reading the hell out of my books.

They sell like hotcakes.

So much so that I don't really have to keep teaching, but I do it anyway. Why? I ask myself the same question all the time. To keep up appearances? Because I truly do love the kids?

Or, maybe it's because I know that if I wrote all the time, I would eventually truly, completely succumb to my fantasy worlds and just live there.

I'd go insane.

Writing has always been an outlet for me. I've been keeping diaries since I was a little girl, and I still keep one.

But it can also be dangerous for me. I'm too fantastical, as my mother used to put it. I get too wrapped up in my imagination and can't separate what's real from what's fantasy.

Teaching, having a "normal" job keeps me grounded.

But writing frees my soul.

I type out the final sentence of my latest manuscript and adjust my glasses as I peer at the screen critically.

La fin.

No sooner is it over than another plot is bubbling up inside my head.

I sigh. This is how it goes with me. No sooner do I get one idea out than another one is taking its place. Some might say it's a vicious, never-ending cycle.

I quickly jot down the basics of the next story, though I don't do a strict outline. I'm not a rigid plotter. I let the story unfold before me. I let the characters lead me. It's like embarking on a journey with new friends, and I'm oftentimes just as surprised as the readers to find out where the characters take me.

For me, writing is like interactively reading a book.

I spend the next hour jumping into chapter one, and by the time I finally still my typing fingers, I see that it's way later than a teacher should be up on a school night.

I sigh and close my laptop before I remove my glasses and run a hand through my hair.

My mind is still buzzing, the characters braying at me, wanting to get their stories out, but I try to calm the chaos within me with some deep breathing exercises that are supposed to quiet the mind.

I push my pajama bottoms off so I'm left only in my panties and a cami. Then, I crawl under the covers and let exhaustion overtake me.

Chapter 3

Zane

I stiffen within my jeans when I see her the next morning. Christ, but she dresses more like a sexy secretary than an elementary school teacher. I never had such a hot little piece for a teacher in grade school, anyway.

My eyes sweep her from head to toe, taking in the navy pencil skirt and sky blue button-up she's wearing. The color of her top perfectly matches her eyes. It enhances them, making them appear even lighter behind those tortoiseshell frames that only bring out the hint of gold in her hair.

Next, I scan her shapely calves, my eyes falling down to rest on the sensible navy pumps she's wearing. They're classic and close-toed with a nice heel but nothing too outrageous. How I'd love to caress her calves, those legs thrown over my shoulder, those shoes on her feet as I drive deep within her, making her mine.

Mine. She should be *mine.*

That familiar ache of longing lodges deep in my chest, and I take in a shaky breath as I begin to follow along behind her—at a distance of course.

This is our weekday morning ritual. I meet her like this and walk her to school. She doesn't live far from the institution she works at, but there's no way in hell I'm taking any chances with her safety. I shadow her every step of the way to make sure no one messes with her.

I'd burn this whole city to the ground if someone hurt her. I'm not being dramatic either. I'm motherfucking serious. One hair on her head gets harmed, and I'll blow this whole place up.

So, really I'm doing a human service by following her and making sure she's okay.

Once she's safely inside the building, I retreat to a more secluded location in the park near the school. I lounge on my usual bench with my legs stretched out in front of me and pull up my feeds inside the school.

Yeah, I know it's illegal to bug a school, but ask me if I give a fuck.

I only bugged her classroom. I can tap into the cameras already in the hall-ways and common areas, but the school doesn't have any cameras in the teach-ers' individual classrooms, and I can't very well leave Anne alone all that time.

I can't stop the smile that pulls at the corners of my lips as I watch her teaching her students. She smiles at them kindly, and there's a light in her eyes as she pays each student individual attention.

It's obvious from the adoring way they look up at her that they worship her. And I can't say I really blame them. I worship her too.

She takes them through math, English, and social studies, and then the bell rings for lunch.

I watch her walk over to her little personal fridge where she keeps some premade salads and fruit. It pleases me to no end that she mostly chooses to stay in her room and eat her lunch alone rather than join the other teachers in the teacher's lounge.

I grab an apple out of my own pocket and take a bite out of it, sharing this lunchtime with her.

My hand tightens on the fruit when a knock sounds on her door. I frown, pissed off that someone is interrupting our time together.

She walks over to the door to see who it is, and I drop my apple, my vision blurring red for a moment, when I see the pompous fucker on the other side of the door.

"Ron," she greets him in surprise.

"Hello, Anne," he purrs as he leans in her doorway.

My lip curls up into a sneer.

"Can I help you?" she asks in confu-sion. She makes no move to step back and allow him entry into her classroom, and I mentally cheer her. *Good girl.*

"Actually, you can," he practically croons down at her. It couldn't be more obvious what the fucker really wants. He was just hired last week, and I've had my eye on him. Something about the way he looked at my Annie the first time he saw her told me he was going to be a problem.

"I packed way too much lunch and wondered if you'd like to share it with me."

Anne looks surprised, but then she smiles at him. My anger flares up at her smiling at any man. I'm partially molli-fied when she shakes her head, though. "I'm sorry, Ron, but I've already got lunch." She motions over to her desk where her half-eaten salad sits.

I glance back at the fucker smugly. *There. Take that. She's clearly not interested.*

To my mortification, he pushes off her doorway and pushes his way into the room, brushing his body against hers before she has a chance to fully step back and give him entry.

"That's okay," he says, "Mind if I just keep you company then?"

She frowns for a moment, but then she schools her features and relents, "Okay."

She's too damn nice, my Annie. She doesn't do well with saying no to people, never wanting to hurt anyone's feelings.

I grit my teeth as the prick pulls a chair right up next to hers behind her desk.

I damn near cheer when I see her sit gracefully in her own chair and roll it a bit away from him, though. *Good girl.*

At first, she seems to just suffer through it—politely of course. She glances longingly at her computer screen, though. I know her fingers are itching to type out more of the story she's currently working on.

Something this guy would never understand about her. But I do. God, I do. I understand everything about her. And while I've never been a big romance novel reader, I read every one Anne publishes.

Because it's a part of *her*. *She* wrote it. It came straight from her imagination. Her innermost thoughts.

And Christ what an imagination she has. I'm unashamed to admit that I've stroked off many a night to the dirty scenarios she comes up with in her books, only in my mind the heroine is replaced with her and the hero with me.

Anne might not have any firsthand knowledge of sex, but I know what she wants, what she fantasizes about. It's all there in her books like a sexual map to her pleasure.

And God how I would love to give it all to her, take her to the heights of plea-sure she fantasizes about.

At some point, the fucker begins wearing down on her. I clench my teeth. He's beginning to charm her. I notice her smiling more. My stomach drops as her smiles become more genuine and she laughs, a light tinkling of bells.

Hot jealousy spears my stomach. She *laughed* for him. I feel irrationally betrayed. She doesn't even know I exist, yet I feel the knife of betrayal sink deep into my gut that she laughed for another man.

He's grinning back at her stupidly, his chest puffed out like a proud peacock preening for a female.

Idiot.

My hands shake with murderous rage as I study him.

Sandy blond hair, brown eyes, muscular build. I suppose women might find him attractive. He's not as tall or muscular as I am. I can guarantee you that.

Anne laughs again, the sound bubbling up from her chest. His eyes drop down to her chest and darken with lust.

Mine darken with rage.

He lays his hand atop hers where it sits on her desk.

That's it. This fucker is dead.

As much as I feel the need to lash out at something, I fight the urge and force myself to watch the rest of their interaction until lunch is over and he leaves.

Good thing for him he doesn't touch her again.

When the students file back into her room, I finally close out of the feed and stand abruptly.

I make my way over to the gym

where I train and head straight for the punching bags.

I've got to work some of this aggression out before I explode.

My jaw is clenched so tightly my teeth ache.

I hit the bag over and over again until I'm dripping with sweat.

I can't get the image of his hand on hers out of my head.

Every time I think of it, I pound the bag with renewed vigor.

Finally, I calm enough to think.

And I suddenly know what I have to do.

It's time for Anne to meet me.